Edward the Blue Engine

THE REV. W. AWDRY

WITH ILLUSTRATIONS BY
C. REGINALD DALBY

RANDOM HOUSE New York

Thomas the Tank Engine & Friends

GULLANE

Based on The Railway Series by the Rev. W. Awdry
Copyright © Gullane (Thomas) LLC 2003
All rights reserved under International and Pan-American Copyright Conventions.
Published in the United States by Random House Children's Books,
a division of Random House, Inc., New York, and simultaneously
in Canada by Random House of Canada Limited, Toronto.
Originally published in Great Britain in 1954 as Book 9 in The Railway Series.
First published in this edition in Great Britain in 1999 by Egmont Books Limited.
ISBN: 0-375-82407-3   Library of Congress Control Number: 2002110426
PRINTED IN ITALY   10 9 8 7 6 5 4 3 2 1
www.randomhouse.com/kids
www.thomasthetankengine.com
RANDOM HOUSE and colophon are registered trademarks of Random House, Inc.

DEAR FRIENDS,

I think most of you are fond of Edward. His Driver and Fireman, Charlie Sand and Sidney Hever, are fond of him too. They were very pleased when they knew I was giving Edward a book all to himself.

Edward is old, and some of the other engines were rude about the clanking noise he made as he did his work.

They aren't rude now! These stories tell you why.

THE AUTHOR

Cows

E dward the Blue Engine was getting old. His bearings were worn, and he clanked as he puffed along. He was taking twenty empty cattle trucks to a market town.

The sun shone, the birds sang, and some cows grazed in a field by the line.

"Come on! Come on! Come on!" puffed Edward.

"Oh! Oh! Oh! Oh!" screamed the trucks. Edward puffed and clanked. The trucks rattled and screamed. The cows were not used to trains. The noise and smoke disturbed them.

They twitched up their tails and ran.

They galloped across the field, broke through the fence, and charged the train between the thirteenth and fourteenth trucks. The coupling broke, and the last seven trucks left the rails. They were not damaged, and stayed upright. They ran for a short way along the sleepers before stopping.

Edward felt a jerk but didn't take much notice.

He was used to trucks.

"Bother those trucks!" he thought.

"Why can't they come quietly?" He ran

on to the next station before either he or his Driver
realized what had happened.

When Gordon and Henry heard about the accident, they laughed and laughed. "Fancy allowing cows to break his train! They wouldn't dare do that to us. We'd show them!" they boasted.

Edward pretended not to mind, but Toby was cross.

"You couldn't help it, Edward," he said. "They've never met cows. I have, and I know the trouble they are."

Some days later Gordon rushed through Edward's station.

"Poop, poop!" he whistled. "Mind the cows!"

"Haha, haha, haha!" he chortled, panting up the hill.

"Hurry, hurry, hurry!" puffed Gordon.

"Don't make such a fuss! Don't make such a fuss!"

grumbled his coaches. They rumbled over the viaduct and roared through the next station.

A long, straight stretch of line lay ahead. In the distance was a bridge. It had high parapets on each side.

It seemed to Gordon that there was something on the bridge. His Driver thought so too. "Whoa, Gordon!" he said, and shut off steam.

"Pooh!" said Gordon. "It's only a cow!"

"Shoo! Shoo!" he hissed, moving slowly onto the bridge.

But the cow wouldn't "shoo"! She had lost her calf and felt lonely.

"Moooo!" she said sadly, walking toward him. Gordon stopped!

His Driver, Fireman, and some passengers tried to send her away, but she wouldn't go, so they gave it up.

Presently Henry arrived with a train from the other direction.

"What's this?" he said grandly. "A cow? I'll soon settle her. Be off! Be off!" he puffed. But the cow turned and "mooed" at him. Henry backed away. "I don't want to hurt her," he said.

Drivers, Firemen, and
passengers again tried to move
the cow, but failed. Henry's
Guard went back and put
detonators on the line to protect
his train. At the nearest station he
told them about the cow.

"That must be Bluebell," said a porter thoughtfully.
"Her calf is here, ready to go to market. We'll take it along."

So they unloaded the calf and took it to the bridge.

"Moo! Moo!" wailed the calf.

"Moo! Moo!" bellowed Bluebell.

She nuzzled her calf happily, and the porter led them away.

The two trains started.

"Not a word."

"Keep it dark," whispered Gordon and Henry as they passed; but the story soon spread.

"Well, well, well!" chuckled Edward. "Two big engines afraid of one cow!"

"Afraid —— Rubbish," said Gordon huffily. "We didn't want the poor thing to hurt herself by running against us. We stopped so as not to excite her. You see what I mean, my dear Edward."

"Yes, Gordon," said Edward gravely.

Gordon felt somehow that Edward "saw" only too well.

 # Bertie's Chase

"*P eep! Peep!* We're late," fussed Edward. "*Peep! Peeppipeep!* Where is Thomas? He doesn't usually make us wait."

"Oh dear, what can the matter be? . . . ," sang the Fireman, "Johnnie's so long at . . ."

"Never you mind about Johnnie," laughed the Driver, "just you climb on the cab and look for Thomas. . . . Can you see him?"

"No," the Fireman answered.

The Guard looked at his watch. "Ten minutes late!" he said to the Driver. "We can't wait here all day."

"Look again, Sid," said the Driver, "just in case." "Can you see him?" "Not Thomas," answered the Fireman, "but there's Bertie bus in a tearing hurry. No need to bother with him, though. Likely he's on a Coach Tour or something."

He clambered down.

"Right away, Charlie," said the
Guard, and Edward puffed off.

"*Toooot! Toooot!* Stop! Stop!"
wailed Bertie, roaring into the
yard, but it was no
good. Edward's

last coach had disappeared into
the tunnel.

"Bother!" said Bertie. "Bother Thomas' Fireman not coming to work today. Oh why did I promise to help the passengers catch the train?"

"That will do, Bertie," said his Driver. "A promise is a promise and we must keep it."

"I'll catch Edward or bust," said Bertie grimly as he raced along the road.

"Oh my gears and axles!" he groaned, toiling up the hill. "I'll never be the same bus again!"

"*Tootootoo Tootoot!* I see him. Hurray! Hurray!" he cheered as he reached the top of the hill.

"He's reached the station,"
Bertie groaned the next minute.

"No . . . he's stopped by
a signal. Hurray! Hurray!"
Bertie tore down the hill,
his brakes squealing at
the corners.

His passengers bounced like balls in a bucket. "Well done,
Bertie," they shouted. "Go! Go!"

Hens and dogs scattered in all directions as Bertie raced
through the village.

"Wait! Wait!" he tooted, skidding into the yard.

He was just in time to see the signal drop, the Guard wave his flag, and Edward puff out of the station.

His passengers rushed to the platform, but it was no good, and they came bustling back.

"I'm sorry," said Bertie unhappily.

"Never mind, Bertie," they said. "After him quickly. Third time lucky, you know!"

"Do you think we'll catch him at the next station, Driver?"

"There's a good chance," he answered.
"Our road keeps close to the line,
and we can climb hills better
than Edward."
    He thought for a minute.
"I'll just make sure."
He then spoke to the
Stationmaster while
the passengers waited
impatiently in the bus.

"This hill is too steep! This hill is too steep!" grumbled the coaches as Edward snorted in front.

They reached the top at last and ran smoothly into the station.

"Peepeep!" whistled Edward.

"Get in quickly, please."

The porters and people
hurried and
Edward
impatiently
waited to start.

"Peeeep!" whistled the
Guard, and Edward's Driver looked
back; but the flag didn't wave. There was a distant
"Tooootoooot!" and the Stationmaster, running across,
snatched the green flag out of the Guard's hand.

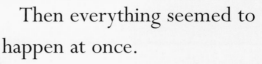

Then everything seemed to happen at once.

"*Too-too-toooooot!*" bellowed Bertie. His passengers poured onto the platform and scrambled into the train. The Stationmaster told the Guard and Driver what had happened, and Edward listened. "I'm sorry about the chase, Bertie," he said.

"My fault," panted Bertie, "late at junction. . . . You didn't know . . . about Thomas' passengers."

"*Peepeep!* Goodbye, Bertie. We're off!" whistled Edward.

"Three cheers for Bertie!" called the passengers. They cheered and waved till they were out of sight.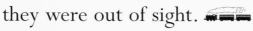

Saved from Scrap

There is a scrap yard near Edward's station. It is full of rusty old cars and machinery. They are brought there to be broken up. The pieces are loaded into trucks, and Edward pulls them to the Steelworks, where they are melted down and used again.

One day Edward saw a traction engine in the yard. "Hullo!" he said. "You're not broken and rusty. What are *you* doing there?"

"I'm Trevor," said the traction engine sadly. "They are going to break me up next week."

"What a shame!" said Edward.

"My Driver says I only need some paint, Brasso, and oil to be as good as new," Trevor went on sadly. "But it's no good. My Master doesn't want me. I suppose it's because I'm old-fashioned."

Edward snorted indignantly. "People say I'm old-fashioned, but I don't care. Sir Topham Hatt says I'm a Useful Engine."

"My Driver says I'm useful too," replied Trevor. "I sometimes feel ill, but I don't give up like these tractors; I struggle on and finish the job. I've never broken down in my life," he ended proudly.

"What work did you do?" asked Edward kindly.

"My Master would send us from farm to farm. We threshed the corn, hauled logs, sawed timber, and did lots of other work. We made friends at all the farms and saw them every year. The children loved to see us come. They followed us in crowds and watched us all day long. My Driver would sometimes give them rides."

Trevor shut his eyes ———
remembering ———

"I like children," he said simply. "Oh yes, I like children."

"Broken up, what a shame! Broken up, what a shame!" clanked Edward as he went back to work. "I *must* help Trevor. I *must*!"

He thought of the people he knew who liked engines.

Edward had lots of friends, but strangely none of them
had room for a traction engine at home!

"It's a shame! It's a
shame!" he hissed as he
brought his coaches to
the station.

Then —— *"Peep! Peep!"*
he whistled. "Why didn't I think of him before?"

Waiting there on the platform was the very person.

It was the Vicar.

"Morning, Charlie. Morning, Sid. Hullo, Edward, you look upset! What's the matter, Charlie?" he asked the Driver.

"There's a traction engine in the scrap yard, Vicar," the Driver said. "He'll be broken up next

week, and it's a shame. Jem Cole says
he never drove a better engine."

"Do save him, sir! You've got
room, sir!" Edward said.

"Yes, Edward, I've
got room," laughed the Vicar, "but I
don't need a traction engine!"

"He'll saw wood and give children
rides. Do buy him, sir, please!"

"We'll see," said the Vicar, and
climbed into the train.

Jem Cole came on Saturday afternoon. "The Reverend's coming to see you, Trevor. Maybe he'll buy you."

"Do you think he will?" asked Trevor hopefully.

"He will when I've lit your fire and cleaned you up," said Jem.

When the Vicar and his two boys arrived in the evening, Trevor was blowing off steam. He hadn't felt so happy for months.

"Watch this, Reverence," called Jem, and Trevor chuffered happily about the yard.

"Oh, Daddy, do buy him," pleaded the boys, jumping up and down in their excitement.

"Now *I'll* try," said the Vicar, climbing up beside Jem. "Show your paces, Trevor," he said, and drove him about the yard. Then he went into the office and came out smiling. "I got him cheap, Jem, cheap."

"D'ye hear that, Trevor?" cried Jem.
"The Reverend's saved you, and
you'll live at the
Vicarage now."

"Peep! Peep!" whistled
Trevor happily.

"Will you drive him home for me, Jem,
and take these scallywags with you? They
won't want to come in the car when there's
a traction engine to ride on!"

Trevor's home in the Vicarage Orchard is close to the railway, and he sees Edward every day. His paint is spotless and his brass shines like gold.

He saws firewood in winter, and Jem sometimes borrows him when a tractor fails. Trevor likes doing his old jobs, but his happiest day is the Church Fête. Then, with a long wooden seat bolted to his bunker, he chuffers round the Orchard giving rides to children.

Long afterward you will see him shut his eyes — remembering.

"I like children," he whispers happily.

Old Iron

One day James had to wait at Edward's station till Edward and his train came in. This made him cross. "Late again!" he shouted.

Edward only laughed, and James fumed away.

"Edward is impossible," he grumbled to the others. "He clanks about like a lot of old iron, and he is so slow he makes us wait."

Thomas and Percy were indignant. "Old iron!" they

snorted. "Slow! Why, Edward could beat you in a race
any day!"

"Really!" said James huffily. "I should like to see
him do it."

One day James' Driver did not feel well when he came to work. "I'll manage," he said. But when they reached the top of Gordon's Hill, he could hardly stand.

The Fireman drove the train to the next station.

He spoke to the Signalman, put the trucks in a siding, and uncoupled James ready for shunting.

Then he helped the Driver over to the station and asked them to look after him and find a "Relief."

Suddenly the Signalman shouted, and the Fireman turned round and saw James puffing away.

He ran hard but he couldn't catch James, and he soon came back to the signal box. The Signalman was busy. "All traffic halted," he announced at last. "Up and down, main lines are clear for thirty miles, and the Inspector's coming."

The Fireman mopped his face.

"What happened?" he asked.

"Two boys were on the footplate. They tumbled off when James started. I shouted at them and they ran like rabbits."

"Just let me catch them," said the Fireman grimly.
"I'll teach them to meddle with my engine."

Both men jumped as the telephone rang. "Yes," answered the Signalman, "he's here. . . . Right, I'll tell him."

"The Inspector's coming at once in Edward. He wants a shunter's pole and a coil of wire rope."

"What for?" wondered the Fireman.

"Search me! But you'd better get them quickly."

The Fireman was ready and waiting when Edward arrived. The Inspector saw the pole and rope. "Good man," he said. "Jump in."

"We'll catch him, we'll catch him," puffed Edward, crossing to the up line in pursuit.

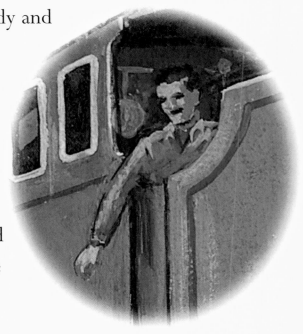

James was laughing as he left the yard.
"What a lark! What a lark!" he chuckled
to himself.

Presently he missed his Driver's hand on the regulator . . .
and then he realized there was no one in his cab. . . .

"What shall I do?" he wailed. "I can't stop. Help! Help!"

"We're coming, we're coming!"

Edward was panting up behind with every ounce of steam
he had. With a great effort, he caught up, and crept
alongside, slowly gaining till his smokebox was level with
James' buffer beam.

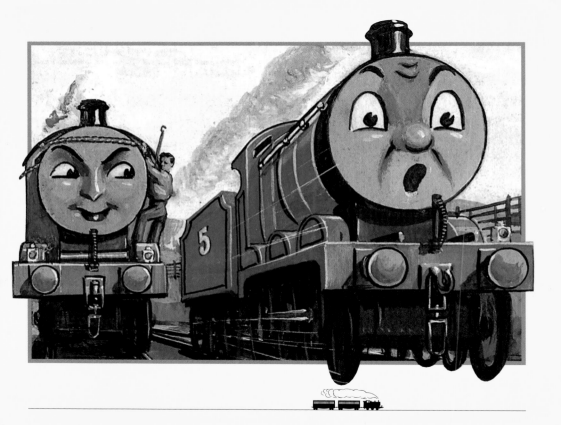

"Steady, Edward."

The Inspector stood on Edward's front, holding a noose of rope in the crook of the shunter's pole. He was trying to slip it over James' buffer. The engines swayed and lurched. He tried again and again. More than once he nearly fell, but just saved himself.

At last — "Got him!" he shouted. He pulled the noose tight and came back to the cab safely.

Gently braking, so as not to snap the rope, Edward's Driver checked the engines' speed, and James' Fireman scrambled across and took control.

The engines puffed back side by side. "So the 'old iron' caught you after all!" chuckled Edward.

"I'm sorry," whispered James. "Thank you for saving me."

"That's all right."

"You were splendid, Edward."

Sir Topham Hatt was waiting, and thanked the men warmly. "A fine piece of work," he said. "James, you can rest, and then take your train. I'm proud of you, Edward. You shall go to the Works, and have your worn parts mended."

"Oh! Thank you, sir!" said Edward happily. "It'll be *lovely* not to clank."

The two naughty boys were soon caught by the police, and their fathers walloped them soundly.

They were also forbidden to watch trains till they could be trusted.

James' Driver soon got well in the hospital and is now back at work. James missed him very much, but he missed Edward more. And you will be glad to know that when Edward came home the other day, James and all the other engines gave him a tremendous welcome.

Sir Topham Hatt thinks he will be deaf for weeks!

OTHER TITLES IN
THE RAILWAY SERIES

Gordon the Big Engine

Henry the Green Engine

James the Red Engine

Percy the Small Engine

Really Useful Engines

Tank Engine Thomas Again

Thomas the Tank Engine

The Three Railway Engines

Toby the Tram Engine